T0134809

Al the Alligator Loves to Read

AuthorHouse™
1663 Liberty Drive
Bloomington, IN 47403
www.authorhouse.com
Phone: 1 (800) 839-8640

Published by AuthorHouse 09/14/2018

ISBN: 978-1-5462-5842-1 (sc)
ISBN: 978-1-5462-5843-8 (e)

Library of Congress Control Number: 2018910364

Print information available on the last page.

This book is printed on acid-free paper.

authorHOUSE®

Al the Alligator Loves to Read

BY
LU TREJO

ILLUSTRATED BY
DANIELLA CALLIHAM

Al the Alligator loves to read.
And read and read
and read indeed.

He read cookbooks and
school books and menus too.

MENU
DRINKS
$3.99
$3.99
$3.99
Breakfast
$8.99
$10.99
$4.99
$5.99
MENU
LUNCH/DINNER
$7.99
$4.99

He even read books about
building canoes.

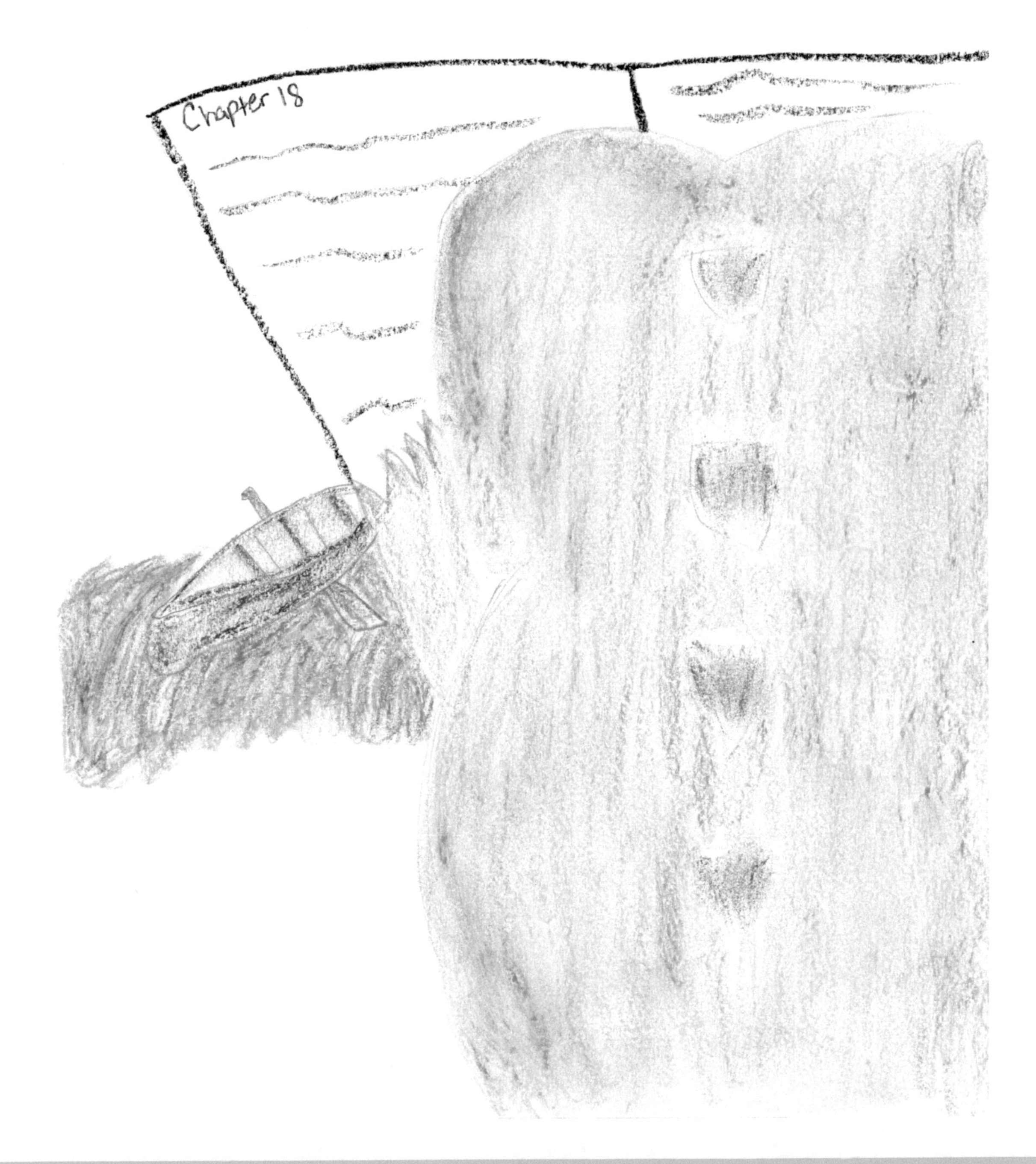
Chapter 18

He read in the morning....

on his breaks...

and on the sidewalk too...

in the park and on the bus...

Public
Transport

standing in line and
in elevators too.

Floor 3

He even read books with
his best friend, Stu.

He cooked dinner with a book and
brushed his teeth with one too.

Meat
Balls

And when he turned off the lights, his books were there too.

Book Paradise

Al could never get enough of his favorite thing - BOOKS!

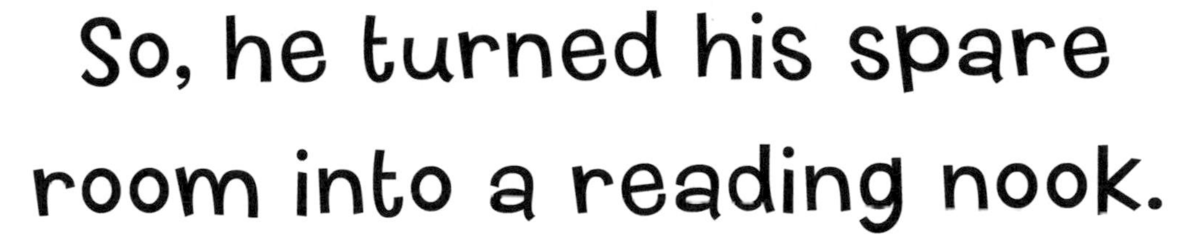

So, he turned his spare room into a reading nook.

All his friends would come
over and trade him for theirs,
and all could keep reading
because everyone shared.

THE END.

Printed in the United States
By Bookmasters